Fun With Homophones

Stephanie Matschke

PAGE PUBLISHING
Conneaut Lake, PA

First originally published by Page Publishing 2023

ISBN 979-8-88960-517-1 (pbk)
ISBN 979-8-88960-530-0 (digital)

Printed in the United States of America

Acknowledgments

Heartfelt gratitude goes to my daughter Marti and my granddaughter, Olivia, for the unwavering interest and time they devoted to this project. And an abundance of appreciation is due to my daughter Karen for her enthusiastic support and contributions. Many, many thanks also go to Phyllis, my friend and helper, for keeping the project on track and my head above water while taking care of countless tasks crucial to the success of this project.

Introduction

Let's have some fun with homophones—those fascinating little features of our language that are made up of two or more words that sound exactly alike but do not have the same spelling or the same meaning.

As the chief instigator of this undertaking—creating a matching game that highlights homophones—and as the primary source of the homophones to be used, I hope this dabbling into a small treasure of words will lead you to a place of delight in discovering new—and, dare I say, exciting—words to embrace as newfound friends while also relishing the meeting up with all acquaintances, maybe half forgotten.

By the way, none of the homophones in this book include words that begin with a capital letter (proper nouns and proper adjectives) or words with internal punctuation, such as hyphens, apostrophes, and accent marks.

So now let's take a quick look at how this book works so you can dive right in and *enjoy*.

The book is divided into two sections. Section 1 consists of forty numbered lists of words—ten words per list. Immediately following each word is a number in parentheses indicating the number of homophones you will want to come up with. Then the blank line provides a place to write your "answers."

Section 2 consists of all the correct homophones numbered to correspond with the numbered lists of words in the first section.

Now you can see how your homophones stack up and congratulate yourself or ready yourself for your next try. But most important of all is this: have fun!

Section 1

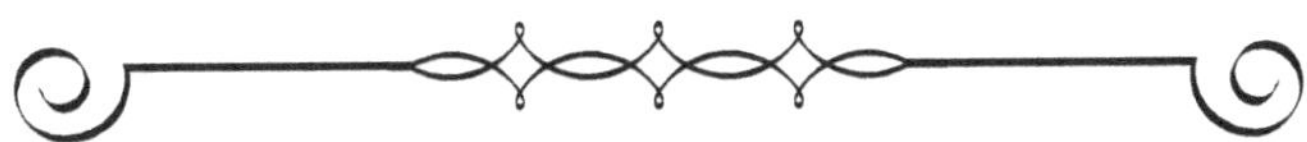

Words

List 1

1. nice (1)   : ________________________

2. symbol (1)   : ________________________

3. brows (1)   : ________________________

4. copes (1)   : ________________________

5. surf (1)   : ________________________

6. fawn (1)   : ________________________

7. slough (1)   : ________________________

8. plat (1)   : ________________________

9. brews (1)   : ________________________

10. wave (1)   : ________________________

List 2

1. suede (1) : _______________________

2. chard (1) : _______________________

3. trimmer (1) : _______________________

4. axe (1) : _______________________

5. grip (1) : _______________________

6. bomb (1) : _______________________

7. brewed (1) : _______________________

8. time (1) : _______________________

9. clamor (1) : _______________________

10. prior (1) : _______________________

List 3

1. bowl (2)   : ____________, ___________

2. heart (1)   : ________________________

3. berry (1)   : ________________________

4. mustard (1)   : ______________________

5. cash (1)   : ________________________

6. liken (1)   : ________________________

7. idol (2)   : ___________, ___________

8. want (1)   : ________________________

9. rain (2)   : ___________, ___________

10. towed (1)   : ________________________

List 4

1. sword (1) : _______________________

2. loop (1) : _______________________

3. weather (2) : ___________, ___________

4. gamble (1) : _______________________

5. key (1) : _______________________

6. chased (1) : _______________________

7. muscles (1) : _______________________

8. click (1) : _______________________

9. presents (1) : _______________________

10. metal (3) : ___________, ___________,

____

List 5

1. pistol (1) : ________________________________

2. levee (1) : ________________________________

3. dingy (1) : ________________________________

4. sees (2) : ______________, ______________

5. hanger (1) : ________________________________

6. clack (1) : ________________________________

7. alter (1) : ________________________________

8. hoard (1) : ________________________________

9. hue (1) : ________________________________

10. you (2) : ____________, ______________

List 6

1. beer (1)   : ______________________________

2. freeze (2)   : ____________, ____________

3. rigor (1)   : ______________________________

4. coral (1)   : ______________________________

5. barred (1)   : ______________________________

6. lee (1)   : ______________________________

7. nickers (1)   : ______________________________

8. petal (2)   : ____________, ____________

9. moat (1)   : ______________________________

10. bin (1)   : ______________________________

List 7

1. fro (1)   : _______________________________

2. locks (2)   : _______________, _______________

3. rumor (1)   : _______________________________

4. corral (1)   : _______________________________

5. kernel (1)   : _______________________________

6. coal (2)   : _______________, _______________

7. palette (2)   : _______________, _______________

8. nay (1)   : _______________________________

9. sleigh (1)   : _______________________________

10. rude (1)   : _______________________________

List 8

1. adds (2) : _______________, _______________

2. burrow (2) : _______________, _______________

3. humorous (1) : _______________________________

4. gin (1) : _______________________________

5. marshal (1) : _______________________________

6. straight (1) : _______________________________

7. right (3) : _______________, _______________,

____

8. dental (1) : _______________________________

9. cent (2) : _______________, _______________

10. muse (1) : _______________________________

List 9

1. foe (1) : _______________________________

2. collard (1) : _______________________________

3. mule (1) : _______________________________

4. canvas (1) : _______________________________

5. faint (1) : _______________________________

6. jam (1) : _______________________________

7. cents (3) : _____________, _____________, _______________________

8. cruise (1) : _______________________________

9. links (1) : _______________________________

10. flocks (1) : _______________________________

List 10

1. seed (1) : _______________________

2. row (1) : _______________________

3. cruel (1) : _______________________

4. sane (1) : _______________________

5. missile (1) : _______________________

6. surge (1) : _______________________

7. pearl (1) : _______________________

8. sorry (1) : _______________________

9. born (1) : _______________________

10. troop (1) : _______________________

List 11

1. cousin (1) : ________________________

2. sight (2) : _____________, ___________

3. hostile (1) : ________________________

4. canter (1) : ________________________

5. taper (1) : ________________________

6. dual (1) : ________________________

7. rye (1) : ________________________

8. core (1) : ________________________

9. ensure (1) : ________________________

10. lean (1) : ________________________

List 12

1. sender (1) : _______________________________

2. coy (1) : _______________________________

3. facial (1) : _______________________________

4. heir (2) : _____________, _____________

5. plural (1) : _______________________________

6. comedy (1) : _______________________________

7. yolk (1) : _______________________________

8. phrase (1) : _______________________________

9. bar (1) : _______________________________

10. waddle (1) : _______________________________

List 13

1. summary (1)   : _______________________________

2. buckle (1)   : _______________________________

3. spayed (1)   : _______________________________

4. taught (1)   : _______________________________

5. meat (2)   : _____________, _____________

6. rue (1)   : _______________________________

7. cause (1)   : _______________________________

8. title (1)   : _______________________________

9. stayed (1)   : _______________________________

10. grizzly (1)   : _______________________________

List 14

1. guilds (1) : _________________________

2. quints (1) : _________________________

3. laps (1) : _________________________

4. review (1) : _________________________

5. utter (1) : _________________________

6. moose (1) : _________________________

7. pie (1) : _________________________

8. clue (1) : _________________________

9. leech (1) : _________________________

10. woe (1) : _________________________

List 15

1. coo (1)   : _______________________________

2. minks (1)   : _______________________________

3. compliment (1)   : _______________________________

4. flare (1)   : _______________________________

5. lintel (1)   : _______________________________

6. tender (1)   : _______________________________

7. tool (1)   : _______________________________

8. imminent (1)   : _______________________________

9. flew (2)   : _______________, _______________

10. ode (1)   : _______________________________

List 16

1. miner (1) : _______________________

2. gaffe (1) : _______________________

3. cereal (1) : _______________________

4. shoe (2) : _____________, _____________

5. liar (1) : _______________________

6. nave (1) : _______________________

7. throws (1) : _______________________

8. booty (1) : _______________________

9. discreet (1) : _______________________

10. birth (1) : _______________________

List 17

1. elicit (1)   : _______________________________

2. eye (1)   : _______________________________

3. away (1)   : _______________________________

4. sucker (1)   : _______________________________

5. immigrant (1)   : _______________________________

6. peek (2)   : _____________, _____________

7. feudal (1)   : _______________________________

8. llama (1)   : _______________________________

9. shoot (1)   : _______________________________

10. cuddle (1)   : _______________________________

List 18

1. bizarre (1) : _______________________________

2. clinch (1) : _______________________________

3. coop (1) : _______________________________

4. dessert (1) : _______________________________

5. bus (1) : _______________________________

6. mantle (1) : _______________________________

7. slight (1) : _______________________________

8. way (2) : _____________, _____________

9. leaf (1) : _______________________________

10. sink (1) : _______________________________

List 19

1. rhyme (1)   : ________________________________

2. chase (1)   : ________________________________

3. him (2)   : ______________, ______________

4. cue (1)   : ________________________________

5. paws (1)   : ________________________________

6. all (1)   : ________________________________

7. sheer (1)   : ________________________________

8. border (1)   : ________________________________

9. flex (1)   : ________________________________

10. bridal (1)   : ________________________________

List 20

1. horse (1) : _______________________

2. fryer (1) : _______________________

3. bell (1) : _______________________

4. braise (1) : _______________________

5. sweet (1) : _______________________

6. beau (1) : _______________________

7. coat (1) : _______________________

8. mutter (1) : _______________________

9. tort (1) : _______________________

10. some (1) : _______________________

List 21

1. set (1) : _______________________

2. repel (1) : _______________________

3. lesson (1) : _______________________

4. brim (1) : _______________________

5. claws (1) : _______________________

6. tinsel (1) : _______________________

7. jeans (1) : _______________________

8. packed (1) : _______________________

9. choose (1) : _______________________

10. winch (1) : _______________________

List 22

1. manner (1)   : _______________________

2. gym (1)   : _______________________

3. tic (1)   : _______________________

4. dents (1)   : _______________________

5. done (1)   : _______________________

6. earn (1)   : _______________________

7. serif (1)   : _______________________

8. eves (1)   : _______________________

9. ring (1)   : _______________________

10. hints (1)   : _______________________

List 23

1. mist (1) : _______________________________

2. chilly (2) : _______________, _______________

3. foul (1) : _______________________________

4. loot (1) : _______________________________

5. sacks (1) : _______________________________

6. toll (1) : _______________________________

7. throne (1) : _______________________________

8. tax (1) : _______________________________

9. signet (1) : _______________________________

10. wood (1) : _______________________________

List 24

1. title (1) : _______________________

2. rose (1) : _______________________

3. wrung (1) : _______________________

4. climb (1) : _______________________

5. mints (1) : _______________________

6. model (1) : _______________________

7. veil (2) : _____________, _____________

8. purr (1) : _______________________

9. style (1) : _______________________

10. bough (1) : _______________________

List 25

1. leader (1) : _______________________________

2. parody (1) : _______________________________

3. bolder (1) : _______________________________

4. poll (1) : _______________________________

5. lax (1) : _______________________________

6. reek (1) : _______________________________

7. soul (1) : _______________________________

8. bread (1) : _______________________________

9. mint (1) : _______________________________

10. guilt (1) : _______________________________

List 26

1. slow (1) : _______________________________

2. carrot (3) : _______________, _______________,
____

3. guild (1) : _______________________________

4. sashay (1) : _______________________________

5. plum (1) : _______________________________

6. cannon (1) : _______________________________

7. seller (1) : _______________________________

8. guys (1) : _______________________________

9. lent (1) : _______________________________

10. need (1) : _______________________________

List 27

1. flow (1) : _______________________

2. droop (1) : _______________________

3. might (1) : _______________________

4. rabbit (1) : _______________________

5. maze (1) : _______________________

6. moat (1) : _______________________

7. brain (1) : _______________________

8. principle (1) : _______________________

9. braid (1) : _______________________

10. tents (2) : __________, __________

List 28

1. quartz (1) : _______________________

2. council (1) : _______________________

3. stationary (1) : _______________________

4. staff (1) : _______________________

5. prays (1) : _______________________

6. please (1) : _______________________

7. ark (1) : _______________________

8. trader (1) : _______________________

9. patients (1) : _______________________

10. bite (1) : _______________________

List 29

1. band (1)   : _______________________________

2. stint (1)   : _______________________________

3. worst (1)   : _______________________________

4. navel (1)   : _______________________________

5. fir (1)   : _______________________________

6. allowed (1)   : _______________________________

7. aisle (1)   : _______________________________

8. choir (1)   : _______________________________

9. rues (1)   : _______________________________

10. pray (1)   : _______________________________

List 30

1. eyelet (1)   : _______________________

2. cheap (1)   : _______________________

3. handsome (1)   : _______________________

4. profit (1)   : _______________________

5. chic (1)   : _______________________

6. chauffer (1)   : _______________________

7. night (1)   : _______________________

8. sorted (1)   : _______________________

9. boy (1)   : _______________________

10. rock (1)   : _______________________

List 31

1. skull (1) : _________________________

2. tarot (1) : _________________________

3. brooch (1) : _________________________

4. pique (2) : ___________, ___________

5. aerie (1) : _________________________

6. shown (1) : _________________________

7. gate (1) : _________________________

8. piece (1) : _________________________

9. due (1) : _________________________

10. caddy (1) : _________________________

List 32

1. new (2)   : _____________, _____________

2. oracle (1)   : _____________________________

3. step (1)   : _____________________________

4. dough (1)   : _____________________________

5. mat (1)   : _____________________________

6. wrapped (2)   : _____________, _____________

7. close (1)   : _____________________________

8. ought (1)   : _____________________________

9. wail (1)   : _____________________________

10. morning (1)   : _____________________________

List 33

1. rinse (1)   : _______________________

2. beach (1)   : _______________________

3. saver (1)   : _______________________

4. leased (1)   : _______________________

5. steel (1)   : _______________________

6. shay (1)   : _______________________

7. lens (1)   : _______________________

8. pair (2)   : _____________, _____________

9. limb (1)   : _______________________

10. eek (1)   : _______________________

List 34

1. rough (1)   : _______________________________

2. overseas (1)   : _______________________________

3. tolled (1)   : _______________________________

4. faker (1)   : _______________________________

5. ant (1)   : _______________________________

6. literal (1)   : _______________________________

7. stair (1)   : _______________________________

8. dine (1)   : _______________________________

9. but (1)   : _______________________________

10. by (2)   : _____________, _____________

List 35

1. heroin (1) : _______________________________

2. size (1) : _______________________________

3. holy (2) : _______________, _______________

4. current (1) : _______________________________

5. patty (1) : _______________________________

6. pudding (1) : _______________________________

7. lays (2) : _______________, _______________

8. folds (1) : _______________________________

9. gourd (1) : _______________________________

10. conk (1) : _______________________________

List 36

1. gorilla (1)　　　　: ______________________________

2. hearty (1)　　　　: ______________________________

3. sick (1)　　　　　: ______________________________

4. many (2)　　　　　: ______________, ______________

5. root (1)　　　　　: ______________________________

6. rout (1)　　　　　: ______________________________

7. groan (1)　　　　　: ______________________________

8. tea (1)　　　　　　: ______________________________

9. rack (1)　　　　　: ______________________________

10. chants (1)　　　　: ______________________________

List 37

1. stolen (1) : _____________________________

2. prints (1) : _____________________________

3. vein (2) : _____________, _____________

4. barren (1) : _____________________________

5. pries (1) : _____________________________

6. odder (1) : _____________________________

7. bitter (1) : _____________________________

8. cedar (3) : _____________, _____________,
____

9. lamb (1) : _____________________________

10. tins (1) : _____________________________

List 38

1. worn (1) : _______________________

2. wilds (1) : _______________________

3. grocer (1) : _______________________

4. hurdle (1) : _______________________

5. herd (1) : _______________________

6. burger (1) : _______________________

7. cord (2) : _____________, _____________

8. turn (1) : _______________________

9. creek (1) : _______________________

10. tracked (1) : _______________________

List 39

1. weld (1)   : ________________________________

2. pennants (1)   : ________________________________

3. willed (1)   : ________________________________

4. leaks (1)   : ________________________________

5. false (1)   : ________________________________

6. plotted (1)   : ________________________________

7. use (2)   : ______________, ______________

8. roll (1)   : ________________________________

9. greater (2)   : ______________, ______________

10. reed (1)   : ________________________________

List 40

1. riffs (1)   : _______________________

2. roomy (1)   : _______________________

3. gram (1)   : _______________________

4. spits (1)   : _______________________

5. side (1)   : _______________________

6. trust (1)   : _______________________

7. censor (2)   : ____________, ____________

8. vial (1)   : _______________________

9. caster (1)   : _______________________

10. few (1)   : _______________________

Section 2

Homophones

List 1

1. gneiss

2. cymbal

3. browse

4. copse

5. serf

6. faun

7. slew

8. plait

9. bruise

10. waive

List 2

1. swayed

2. charred

3. tremor

4. acts

5. grippe

6. bombe

7. brood

8. thyme

9. clammer

10. prier

List 3

1. boll, bole

2. hart

3. bury

4. mustered

5. cache

6. lichen

7. idle, idyll

8. wont

9. reign, rein

10. toad

List 4

1. soared

2. loupe

3. wether, whether

4. gambol

5. quay

6. chaste

7. mussels

8. clique

9. presence

10. medal, meddle, mettle

List 5

1. pistil

2. levy

3. dinghy

4. seas, seize

5. hangar

6. claque

7. altar

8. horde

9. hew

10. ewe, yew

List 6

1. bier

2. frieze, frees

3. rigger

4. choral

5. bard

6. lea

7. knickers

8. pedal, peddle

9. mote

10. been

List 7

1. froe

2. lochs, lox

3. roomer

4. chorale

5. colonel

6. kohl, cole

7. pallet, palate

8. neigh

9. slay

10. rued

List 8

1. ads, adze

2. borough, burro

3. humerus

4. jinn

5. martial

6. strait

7. rite, wright, write

8. dentil

9. scent, sent

10. mews

List 9

1. faux

2. collared

3. mewl

4. canvass

5. feint

6. jamb

7. scents, since, sense

8. crews

9. lynx

10. phlox

List 10

1. cede

2. roe

3. crewel

4. seine

5. missal

6. serge

7. purl

8. sari

9. borne

10. troupe

List 11

1. cozen

2. site, cite

3. hostel

4. cantor

5. tapir

6. duel

7. wry

8. corps

9. insure

10. lien

List 12

1. cinder

2. koi

3. fascial

4. ere, err

5. pleural

6. comity

7. yoke

8. frays

9. barre

10. wattle

List 13

1. summery

2. buccal

3. spade

4. taut

5. meet, mete

6. roux

7. caws

8. tidal

9. staid

10. grisly

List 14

1. gills

2. quince

3. lapse

4. revue

5. udder

6. mousse

7. pi

8. clew

9. leach

10. whoa

List 15

1. coup

2. minx

3. complement

4. flair

5. lentil

6. tinder

7. tulle

8. immanent

9. flue, flu

10. owed

List 16

1. minor

2. gaff

3. serial

4. shoo, choux

5. lyre

6. knave

7. throes

8. bootie

9. discrete

10. berth

List 17

1. illicit

2. aye

3. aweigh

4. succor

5. emigrant

6. peak, pique

7. futile

8. lama

9. chute

10. cuttle

List 18

1. bazaar

2. clench

3. coupe

4. desert

5. buss

6. mantel

7. sleight

8. weigh, whey

9. lief

10. synch

List 19

1. rime

2. chaise

3. hem, hymn

4. queue

5. pause

6. awl

7. shear

8. boarder

9. flecks

10. bridle

List 20

1. hoarse

2. friar

3. belle

4. brays

5. suite

6. bow

7. cote

8. mudder

9. torte

10. sum

List 21

1. sett

2. rappel

3. lessen

4. bream

5. clause

6. tensile

7. genes

8. pact

9. chews

10. wench

List 22

1. manor

2. gem

3. tick

4. dense

5. dun

6. urn

7. seraph

8. eaves

9. wring

10. hence

List 23

1. missed

2. chili, chile

3. fowl

4. lute

5. sax

6. tole

7. thrown

8. tacks

9. cygnet

10. would

List 24

1. tidal

2. rows

3. rung

4. clime

5. mince

6. mottle

7. vale, vail

8. per

9. stile

10. bow

List 25

1. liter

2. parity

3. boulder

4. pole

5. lacks

6. wreak

7. sole

8. bred

9. meant

10. gilt

List 26

1. sloe

2. caret, karat, carat

3. gild

4. sachet

5. plumb

6. canon

7. cellar

8. guise

9. lint

10. knead

List 27

1. floe

2. drupe

3. mite

4. rabbet

5. maize

6. mote

7. brane

8. principal

9. brayed

10. tense, tints

List 28

1. quarts

2. counsel

3. stationery

4. staph

5. praise

6. pleas

7. arc

8. traitor

9. patience

10. byte

List 29

1. banned

2. stent

3. wurst

4. naval

5. fur

6. aloud

7. isle

8. quire

9. ruse

10. prey

List 30

1. islet

2. cheep

3. hansom

4. prophet

5. sheikh

6. shofar

7. knight

8. sordid

9. buoy

10. roc

List 31

1. scull

2. taro

3. broach

4. peek, peak

5. airy

6. shone

7. gait

8. peace

9. dew

10. catty

List 32

1. knew, gnu

2. auricle

3. steppe

4. doe

5. matte

6. rapped, rapt

7. clothes

8. aught

9. wale

10. mourning

List 33

1. rents

2. beech

3. savor

4. least

5. steal

6. shea

7. lends

8. pare, pear

9. limn

10. eke

List 34

1. ruff

2. oversees

3. told

4. fakir

5. aunt

6. littoral

7. stare

8. dyne

9. butt

10. bye, buy

List 35

1. heroine

2. sighs

3. holey, wholly

4. currant

5. paddy

6. putting

7. leis, laze

8. foals

9. gored

10. conch

List 36

1. guerilla

2. hardy

3. sic

4. minnie, mini

5. route

6. route

7. grown

8. tee

9. wrack

10. chance

List 37

1. stollen

2. prince

3. vane, vain

4. baron

5. prize

6. otter

7. bidder

8. seeder, ceder, seater

9. lam

10. tends

List 38

1. warn

2. wiles

3. grosser

4. hurtle

5. heard

6. burgher

7. chord, cored

8. tern

9. creak

10. tract

List 39

1. welled

2. penance

3. wield

4. leeks

5. faults

6. plodded

7. ewes, yews

8. role

9. grater, grader

10. read

List 40

1. rifts

2. rheumy

3. graham

4. spitz

5. sighed

6. trussed

7. censer, sensor

8. vile

9. castor

10. phew

About the Author

The author confesses a lifelong infatuation with words—beginning in her early school years with her favorite daily activity of composing sentences, each containing a word from the day's spelling list and eventually culminating with her college studies earning her a degree with a major and two minors in tech writing, journalism, and semasiology. These studies served as the wind to her back in landing a coveted editorial position in her alma mater's office for college publications. Interjecting a bit of levity to the demanding workload, she created many word-for-the-day postings, which included whimsical sketches of feathered and furry critters engaged in a play on words. She thrived in the academic setting, where she remained until retirement. Life is sweet now with family and friends and with Moki, her handsome dude of a cat always at her side. The cherry on the cake, she says, is the publication of this little book of homophones.